tiny titans

Go Camping!

y Art
Baltazar

W9-BGR-836

GROSSET & DUNLAP
AN IMPRINT OF PENGUIN GROUP (USA) INC.

GROSSET & DUNLAP
Published by the Penguin Group
Penguin Group (USA) Inc., 375 Hudson Street, New York, New York 10014, USA
Penguin Group (Canada), 90 Eglinton Avenue East, Suite 700, Toronto, Ontario M4P 2Y3, Canada
(a division of Pearson Penguin Canada Inc.)
Penguin Books Ltd., 80 Strand, London WC2R 0RL, England
Penguin Group Ireland, 25 St. Stephen's Green, Dublin 2, Ireland
(a division of Penguin Books Ltd.)
Penguin Group (Australia), 250 Camberwell Road, Camberwell, Victoria 3124,
Australia (a division of Pearson Australia Group Pty. Ltd.)
Penguin Books India Pvt. Ltd., 11 Community Centre, Panchsheel Park, New Delhi—110 017, India
Penguin Group (NZ), 67 Apollo Drive, Rosedale, North Shore 0632, New Zealand
(a division of Pearson New Zealand Ltd.)
Penguin Books (South Africa) (Pty.) Ltd., 24 Sturdee Avenue, Rosebank,
Johannesburg 2196, South Africa

Penguin Books Ltd., Registered Offices: 80 Strand, London WC2R 0RL, England

Published by Grosset & Dunlap, a division of Penguin Young Readers Group,
345 Hudson Street, New York, New York 10014. GROSSET & DUNLAP
is a trademark of Penguin Group (USA) Inc. Printed in the U.S.A.

Library of Congress Cataloging-in-Publication Data

Baltazar, Art.
Tiny Titans go camping! / written and illustrated by Art Baltazar.
p. cm.
Summary: Classic comic book superheroes, portrayed
as first-graders, go on a fun-filled camping trip.
ISBN 978-0-448-45249-4 (pbk.)
[1. Superheroes--Fiction. 2. Camping--Fiction.] I. Title.
PZ7.B21386Tk 2010
[E]--dc22
2009020851

ISBN 978-0-448-45249-4   10 9 8 7 6 5 4 3 2 1

Meet the . . .

tiny titans

STARFIRE

ROBIN

CYBORG

She's an alien princess. Very naive and free-spirited. She finds the good in others. Has a crush on Robin and thinks he's cute, but so do all the other girls.

(Dick Grayson) The brave and serious leader of the Tiny Titans. Although he is the original Robin, he is very moody. Also, he has secret crushes on Starfire and Barbara Gordon.

Half boy, half robot. Cyborg is always tinkering with mechanical gadgets, often turning them into something else. His battle cry "BOO-YA!" has earned him the nickname "Big Boo-Ya."

RAVEN

The quiet and mysterious little girl. She really likes to experiment with dark magic, which usually turns into bad practical jokes. Mr. Trigon, the substitute teacher, is her father.

BEAST BOY

The green, little boy who can change into any animal he desires. He's a prankster and loves comics. Has a crush on Terra.

AQUALAD

The little boy from the ocean. Has a pet fish named Fluffy. Aqualad can communicate with all forms of sea life.

BUMBLEBEE

The tiniest of the Tiny Titans. Bumblebee buzzes and packs a mighty stinger.

chapter one

It was another beautiful, sunshine-filled day at Sidekick City Elementary. The Tiny Titans sat at their desks and excitedly watched the clock. They were waiting for the bell to ring and their three-day weekend to start.

"Oh, boy! I can't wait for our big camping trip!" exclaimed Robin.

"Me neither," Cyborg said as he reached into his backpack and pulled out a shiny gadget. "It's my ultra hi-tech Directional Locator Compass 3000! It can get you out of any jam you get yourself into. You'll never get lost with this baby!"

"Wow!" said Robin. "Can it be used for crime fighting?"

Robin turned to Aqualad. "So," he asked. "What are you bringing?"

"I'm bringing my fishing pole," Aqualad said with a smile.

"What!?" Robin asked. "But I thought you were against using fishing poles!"

"Not the way I use them," Aqualad explained.

"What about you, Beast Boy?" the Boy
Wonder asked. "What are you bringing to
our camping trip?"

"I'm bringing an extra pair of clean
underwear," Beast Boy said shyly. "I'm going
to need it after what happened last time."

Finally, the bell rang. The substitute
teacher, Mr. Trigon, shouted with
excitement, "See you in the morning!"

"Wow, Raven, your dad is going to chaperone our camping trip," said Starfire. "This is going to be so much fun!"

"C'mon, Raven," Mr. Trigon said. "Let's get home so we can pack our camping gear! Remember to bring the birdseed! Those birds are not going to feed themselves!"

"This is going to be a long weekend," sighed Raven.

chapter two

It was a lovely morning. The birds were chirping and the sun was shining as the school bus pulled into Sidekick City National Park.

"We're here!" Mr. Trigon shouted. "Breathe in the fresh air, kids!"

"The first thing that we need to do," he added, "is pick an area to set up our tents!" He pointed in one direction for the boys' camp and another for the girls'.

"This park is really cool!" Starfire said as she began unpacking. "After we set up our tent, we should find a nice place to have our tea party!"

"Good idea!" Bumblebee added as she reached into her backpack. "Here, I brought some curtains to hang in our tent!"

I gotta get out of here, Raven thought. *A walk in the woods will do me good.*

Meanwhile, at the other campsite, the boys were setting up their tent. Robin pulled a Bat-Hammer from his Utility Belt.

"What's the hammer for, Robin?" Cyborg asked.

"It's to pound the tent spikes into the ground," Robin replied.

"No need for that, my friend," Cyborg said. "I've got something better! Stand back and watch this."

Cyborg reached into his toolbox and pressed a button. Suddenly, the tent popped up—complete and ready for camping!

"Wow, Cyborg! That was pretty cool, and fast, too!" Robin said. "How'd you do it?"

"It's my Ultimate Tent-O-Matic 3000!" said Cyborg.

"That's amazing. Do you have anything in your toolbox that could make an awesome campfire?" Robin asked.

Raven was walking through the woods and heard Robin ask for a campfire.

She whispered her magic words. "Azarath, Metrion, Zinthos!"

Rocks and logs began to circle through the air. They swirled around and then crashed down to form a fire pit. A flicker of flame magically appeared in the air and lit the campfire.

"No, I don't have anything to start a fire," Cyborg said, "but Raven does."

Chapter Three

Later that night, the Titans all sat around the campfire roasting hot dogs. It was a dark and quiet night with billions of twinkling stars lighting the evening sky.

"Hey, could someone pass the mustard?" Robin asked.

"Sure, Robin," Starfire replied as she looked around. "Oops, I forgot the mustard in the tent! I'll be right back."

Starfire stood up and walked over to the girls tent. Suddenly, she heard a roar coming from the woods!

RRROOAR! GGRRROWL!

Starfire screamed and ran back to the campfire. "There's a scary bear just outside our tent! He was big and hairy and green!"

"Green?" asked Robin.

"Bears aren't green, Starfire," he added. "It was probably just your imagination."

Moments later, the second round of hot dogs was being roasted over the fire.

"Hey, could you pass the ketchup?" Aqualad asked.

"Oops, I forgot the ketchup in the tent!" Bumblebee said. "I'll be right back."

As Bumblebee flew to the girls tent, she suddenly heard a roar coming from the woods!

RRROOAR! GGRRROWL!

"There's a scary monster just outside our tent!" screamed Bumblebee. "I think it's Bigfoot!"

"What did he look like?" Robin asked.

"He was big and hairy and . . . green!" Bumblebee replied.

"Green?" Robin asked as the Titans made their way over to the girls tent.

"Well, Robin, I don't see a bear or Bigfoot," said Cyborg. "But I do see a zebra."

"A zebra? In the woods?" Robin replied.
"Zebras are only found in Africa! Wait a
minute . . . a green zebra?"

"BEAST BOY!" yelled Robin.

"Okay, okay," Beast Boy said. "I promise
never to scare you girls again."

Chapter Four

The next morning, at the Tiny Titans campsite, the girls were preparing for their tea party.

"Would you like more tea, Mr. Bunny Rabbit?" Bumblebee asked while holding a little teapot.

"How about you, Mr. Teddy Bear? Would you like another cookie?" Starfire asked the stuffed bear.

Starfire looked around and noticed an empty dish on their blanket. "We have one extra place setting," she said happily. "We should invite Mr. Trigon!"

Starfire turned to Raven and asked, "Hey, Raven, can you—"

But before Starfire could continue, Raven interrupted. "I know. I'll go ask him."

Raven reluctantly stood up and walked over to Mr. Trigon's tent where he was sitting and enjoying a leftover hot dog.

"Dad . . ." said Raven quietly.

"Hello, dear," Mr. Trigon said with a big smile that showed all his teeth. "What can I help you with?" he asked as he took another bite of his hot dog.

"The girls were wondering . . ." Raven quietly continued, "if, um, if you would like to, um, join our tea party."

Mr. Trigon jumped up, and with a huge smile said, "Tea? With me? I WOULD LOVE TO! I always wanted to join a tea party, but no one has ever asked me!"

"I'm starting to see why," Raven muttered under her breath.

Minutes later, the Titan girls and Mr. Trigon were all sitting on their blanket enjoying the tea party.

"More tea, Mr. Trigon?" asked Starfire while holding the teapot.

Mr. Trigon raised his tiny teacup and said, "Oh, absolutely! We should do this more often. These cookies are delicious!" Mr. Trigon laughed as the sounds of chewing, sipping, and laughing filled the air.

chapter Five

While hiking to the lake, Robin noticed a little bird following him.

"Hello, little bird," he said as he continued his hike.

Moments later, more birds began to follow him—robins, to be exact.

"Hmm, robins are following me, and my name is Robin," he said to himself. "That's kind of funny."

As Robin approached the lake, he noticed that not only were robins following him, but a line of ducks, too.

This is starting to get weird, he thought.

While at the lake, swans and cranes joined in the march. Soon there was a long line of birds following Robin's every step.

This is starting to turn into a parade! he thought.

As Robin walked back to camp, more birds followed him. Soon, eagles and hawks were swooping down to join the parade. He looked behind him and then nervously began running.

"I gotta get rid of these birds!" he said, running faster and faster.

"**RAVEN!** You have to help me!" Robin shouted. "Please help me get rid of these birds! I don't know what to do!"

Raven calmly looked at the birds and with a loud belt yelled, "GO AWAY, BIRDS!"

Immediately the robins, hawks, eagles, cranes, and ducks flew away, leaving Robin standing alone.

Robin watched with a smile on his face as Raven walked away. "Whew!" sighed Robin with relief. "That was a close one."

As soon as Raven was out of sight, the robins, eagles, cranes, hawks, ducks, and all kinds of birds returned.

"Um," Robin said, "I think I may have just gone to the birds."

Chapter Six

Beast Boy sat on a tree stump.

"Man, roasting hot dogs sure gave me an appetite," he said as he took a bite of his apple.

As he looked up from his chewing, he saw Aqualad walking with his fishing gear.

"Hey, Aqualad, where are you going with that tackle box and fishing pole?" asked Beast Boy.

"I'm going fishing," said Aqualad.

"Fishing?" asked Beast Boy. "But I thought you didn't like to fish."

"Well, the way I fish is different than the way everybody else fishes. I don't use hooks." Aqualad smiled.

Beast Boy was very confused. "No hooks?" he asked. "Do you use bait?"

"Oh yeah, I use lots of bait," said Aqualad. "C'mon, I'll show you."

At the lake, they sat down on the water's edge. Aqualad opened his tackle box, which was filled with little treats and snacks and bits of food. Aqualad tied a cookie to the end of his fishing pole and used his Aqua-telepathy to call to the fish.

"Hi, Aqualad! How have you been?" asked the little fish, poking their heads out of the water.

"Here's another cookie, fellas," said Aqualad as more fish began to swim to the surface.

Aqualad looked into his tackle box for more snacks but it was empty. "Sorry, guys, that's all the food I have. I'm fresh out," he said.

"Aw, man," said the fish. "But we're still hungry. How about getting us a pizza?"

"A pizza?" asked Aqualad. "Where am I going to get a pizza?"

"There's a pizzeria just about five miles down the road," said the fish. "If you leave now, you should make it back before it gets dark. Go ahead, we'll wait for you!"

One hour later, Aqualad and Beast Boy were at the pizzeria, standing at the counter and waiting to place their order.

Beast Boy shook his head. "Next time, we should have it delivered."

Chapter Seven

Dawn peered over the distant mountains and the dew glistened in the morning light as the sounds of sleeping campers filled the cool, woodsy air.

This quiet, peaceful scene of nature was quickly interrupted by a shouting Mr. Trigon.

"Aw, yeah, Titans! Rise and shine!" he shouted, clanging pots and pans. "Wake up, sleepy heads! Time for breakfast!"

"Breakfast time already?" asked a drowsy Robin. "What time is it?"

"Five AM," yawned Cyborg as he rolled over in his sleeping bag.

"Five AM?" said Aqualad. "The night sure flies by when you stay up late watching the stars."

The Tiny Titans came out of their tents and gathered around the picnic table. Most of them were still groggy with sleepy eyes.

"C'mon, kids!" Mr. Trigon said excitedly as he placed a heaping pile of homemade pancakes on the table. "Dig in!"

The Titans filled their bellies as the smell of breakfast awoke their neighbor from the next campsite.

"Mmmmm," The Ant said, while sniffing the air. "Those pancakes smell delicious."

"Aw, yeah, Titans! Let's eat!" said The Ant.

"Oh no!" shouted Bumblebee. "You can't invite The Ant to a picnic! He'll bring all his ant friends and it will ruin everything!"

"Oh no! Breakfast will be ruined!" cried Starfire.

"They won't eat much," said The Ant. "They're happy just eating crumbs."

"You are so lucky, Raven," said Starfire. "Your dad makes the best pancakes ever!"

"This is nothing," said Raven. "Wait until he does his pancake dance."

At that moment, Mr. Trigon raised his spatula and began to march in place.

"Okay, kids, ready for the pancake dance?" sang Mr. Trigon. "A-one, a-two, a-three . . ."

"Uh-oh, here we go," sighed Raven.

The End!

RoBin's Going CamPing!
Camping Supplies

What should Robin pack in his backpack?